Don't miss out!

Click the button below to receive a Short Story novel By SO-PHIE KENT FREE. There's no charge and no obligation.

[1]

https://game-romance.funnel.heyappjam.com

THE SUCKER PUNCH

First edition. April 22, 2022.

Written by Sophie Kent.

"THE SUCKER PUNCH"

Pink paper in hand, Chris made a triumphant entry into the "Bar à thyme". The "hip hip hip hooray!" of his assembled friends transported him with ease. Finally he felt happy and confident, well surrounded by his real friends.

At home, the reception had been so disappointing. His mother had seemed to him oddly worried, as if worried about his success. It's true that she never trusted him.

His little sister had ignored his success; she had had the license for over a year already.

Frustrated by this hour of glory that he had been waiting for so long, he had felt a surge of rage rise in him. Rage against his parents, one of whom smothered him with advice, the other with reproaches.

Hate also against this little sister, so perfect in the eyes of the parents, when she was only a snobby, always cunning and making fun of him.

In these very special circumstances, Chris felt the injustice of his situation. His parents gladly applauded the successes of this filthy moth, whom they always treated with indulgence. He, in their eyes, was just a clumsy... A nice, slow boy...

But things were finally going to change. Chris felt all this energy in him, this strength, and this taste for speed which overwhelmed him. He knew he was reckless and virile.

He liked to talk about cars with his friends; he liked to attend car races. When the noise of the engines and the strong smell of hot oil enveloped him, his soul became that of a great pilot.

And that day, he had just obtained the official document that would make a decisive turn in his life: the driver's license... HIS license!

Usually, at home, when he said:

- Unfortunately, I don't have my license yet...

Or else:

- As soon as I have my license...

His sister, the slut, took him back:

- You allowed?! As long as you don't have it, it's not yours! Say THE driver's license but don't take ownership of it yet, you've missed it five times!

There you have it, that was the tragedy of Chris Morgan. A car enthusiast who couldn't get the famous pink paper! Of course, driving had never been a problem for him. At home, it was there, innate, pegged to the body. But all this hassle for the code... While everyone knows that it's no longer any use once you've passed the exam!

Chris had missed this shitty code several times! Consequence... Prohibition to pass the driving yet so well controlled. Six times he had presented himself! It had taken him nine years in all... Nine years of chomping at the bit, spoiling his eyesight on books studded with intersections, priority vehicles and speed bumps!

Fortunately, today, all that was just a bad memory. Well warm, at the counter of friendship, he watered the victory with his friends.

- And let the Champagne flow freely, innkeeper!

For the first time perhaps since he had emerged from childhood, Chris felt recognized... A real man as he understood him, well in tune with modern life... In tune with the existence... He was beaming!

Through the steamy window of the bar, his gaze fell on Sebastian's red 4x4. Just like him, his friend liked massive and powerful cars...

But Chris had another idea. And his own idea was to buy an American, a big limousine. He would soon have the means, since the time he was saving! They were just exhibiting very fine second-hand models in a nearby garage and he promised himself to drop by first thing the next day. With the license in hand, the hard part was done!

Sebastian saw the gleam of lust in his boyfriend's eyes. Sébastien Louette was his best friend. A true friend who had always supported and encouraged him in all circumstances. He had even helped him to revise his code, that's to say!

Besides, this unfailing friendship, Chris returned to him well. For example, when Sébastien lost his job, it was Chris who paid for the 4x4 insurance. Now, Sebastian had found a small job and his finances were looking better. But, in spite of everything, Chris knew very well that he still had some overdue bills. And, once again, he was determined to help him, even if it somewhat cut into the budget intended for the fat American.

Just thinking about their beautiful understanding, Chris felt the tears wet his eyelids.

- Let's toast to friendship! He exclaimed, just to get rid of his confusion.

- To friendship and beautiful cars! Sébastien continued, raising his glass.

And both of them, smiling and champagne on their lips, sank into the contemplation of the beautiful chrome and fire Cherokee.

- Let's drink to the women too!

Chris suddenly launched, seeing a pretty blonde humming past the bar, a big cardboard file wedged under her right arm.

And the rest happened naturally. Among friends, it is well known, no need to talk. They understand each other with a gesture, a look. But then, what Sébastien said as he handed him his keys, warmed Chris's heart, erasing all the past frustrations in one fell swoop.

- You know what? I lend you my Cherokee. Go for a little trip, my Chris. You have your license, I trust you. You go around the block, all alone, like a big... Just enough time for us to open a new bottle of roteux!

Chris didn't have to repeat it twice!

There are people having fun, partying. Meanwhile, there are others working. Mélanie Duplat was in this last category. She was a beautiful young blonde woman. Very beautiful and above all very serious... Besides, she was a bailiff. Conscientious and fond of her profession, she managed, by handling with dexterity the carrot and the stick, to close many more files than most of her colleagues.

She felt great that day. She carried under her right arm a cardboard binder on which was spread out, in capital letters, the title "Dossier no 413, Affaire Louette".

It was exactly the type of business she liked. She knew all the details by heart. Three months of late bills, an "all-terrain" type car to be seized.

For the moment, the seizure was only conservatory. But if, as Melanie had hoped, the man didn't settle his debt within a week, we would go to foreclosure pure and simple. A true delight!

Another one who had had the car bigger than his wallet and couldn't pay his credit. Instinctively, Mélanie hated him, as she hated most people and, more particularly, all 4x4 drivers.

Putting on her glasses, Mélanie consulted her suburban map in search of the home of her "client".

- I'm there! It's on the other side of the main road... She exclaimed, spotting the place.

She turned back, looking for a safe passage. She walked with a determined step, humming, to give herself some enthusiasm:

- It's good for him! He's a big macho...

As she passed, she cast a contemptuous look at the drunks who, still leaning on the counter of the "Bar à Thyme", emitted new admiring whistles at her sight.

She arrived at the pedestrian crossing, the road was very wide and the traffic heavy. A luminous panel displayed: "Pedestrians, cross in two stages". Mélanie Duplat was a disciplined girl. Not the crazy type at all! She stopped quietly at the edge of the sidewalk, waiting for the little man in the signal to turn green.

She was still humming, her nose buried in the map of the neighborhood. She didn't see the big red 4x4 Cherokee rushing at full speed, coming zigzagging and cutting straight across the main road diagonally.

Hardly had she begun a gesture... a cry...

Anyway, Chris Morgan did not have the opportunity to know the sound of her voice. He didn't even hear the pretty bailiff's bones crack because he himself had just been ejected and his skull burst against the wall of the garage where such beautiful American limousines were sold.

The license, the permit, the sucker punch.

THE END.

BOXING FOR RENT

To join Sylvain in Paris, Carmen had broken with her parents, defied her brother Diego, left her country. It was barely a year ago.

Today, what remained of their love? She had thought she had met Prince Charming, a young lawyer with a bright future. What derision!

He was a simple small-time crook who hadn't kept any of his promises. She felt so alone, scorned by this man who had only lied to her.

At first, she had accepted everything, his infidelities, his bad mood, his shenanigans. She had tolerated everything as long as he had made the effort to hide his pranks from her. As long as she believed herself loved, she had forgiven, she had hoped. But now it was over.

Ever since he'd become friends with this Sabine, he barely gave her enough to run the house and barely treated her like his servant. Meanwhile, he was leading the high life with this girl even more dishonest than him!

Between them, they skimmed the "pigeons", as they called them laughing. Sylvain granting himself the title of notary and Sabine that of real estate agent, the two accomplices were selling apartments that they did not own!

When they had cheerfully resold the same property, to several "gogos", they disappeared, to repeat their scenario, under another name, in another district.

In the early days of their life together, Carmen, who had difficulty mastering the subtleties of the French language, had really taken Sylvain for a notary's clerk. A few notions of law, vestiges of a year spent in college, allowed him to create the illusion.

But little by little, Carmen had opened her eyes and discovered a truth that she didn't like. He, for his part, understanding that she was no longer so naive, had begun to distrust her.

The more the days passed, the more irritable he became, he rebuffed her for a yes or a no. Now he didn't even bother to hide his affair with Sabine who, under the pretext of talking business, would burst into their house all the time. Carmen would have liked to leave him but, without money, she felt trapped.

The letters sent to her by her brother were her only comfort. He had just bought a small hotel on the Costa Brava and said that she would always be welcome there.

Unfortunately the few pennies she had did not even allow her to fill the tank of her old car! Of course, Diego would have been happy to advance her the money for the trip, but her dignity forbade her from returning to the country empty-handed, when she left proud and conquering!

Looking for a way out, she thought of the cabinet where Sylvain kept his "secret documents". Perhaps she would find a checkbook or a few Euros there? Feverishly, she began to rummage among the cardboard folders.

Too concentrated on her task, she didn't hear the key turn in the lock and jumped when Sylvain's silhouette framed itself in the doorway.

Seeing her scattered files, he flew into a mad rage and snatched the papers from her hands.

- Oh! You're spying on me now! he said, giving him a masterful slap.

Tears in her eyes, rubbing her sore cheek, she looked at him in horror.

Deliberately turning his back on her, Sylvain left the living room. A few moments later, he returned with a briefcase in which he piled up his incriminating files.

- If I can't trust you anymore, from now on I'll store my papers at Sabine's, he murmured between his teeth.

As she didn't answer, he glared at her with a contemptuous air.

- Don't expect me before Friday. Urgent business to settle in the suburbs. I'll give you a call. he simply said, slamming the door.

Of course, he hadn't deigned to leave her any money! As she stood there, a little dazed, staring at the gaping writing desk, a shiny object at the back of the empty cabinet caught her attention. It was a key. The box key where Sylvain parked his car.

Then, for the first time in her life, a dishonest idea germinated in her mind.

- After all, why not use the same method as him?

It was enough to place an ad, make copies of the key, take advantage of Sylvain's absence to show the premises, collect the rents from any prospective client who needs a house to rent.

Carmen remembered a name she had noticed while leafing through Sylvain's files: "Agence Langlois", one of the pseudonyms used by the couple of crooks. She wrote a text bearing the letterhead of this fictitious agency and went to the headquarters of the magazine on which Sylvain was accustomed to placing his ads for real estate sales.

Luckily, the newspaper to appear for the next day was not yet completed and she was able to insert her message "boxing for rent".

She gave the address and suggested visits on the spot the same afternoon of the day of publication of the newspaper.

The employee who recorded the ad agreed to send the invoice to Sylvain. Everything was going well. Carmen then went to a shoemaker where Sylvain, who was very careful, had his shoes resoled regularly.

The man, like any self-respecting shoemaker, also made the "minute keys". Carmen asked him for several replicas of the boxing key and had the bill put on his friend's account.

Everything seemed in order, Carmen had only one fear, it was that all the applicants would come to the appointment at the same time. A few moments of reflection and she imagined a parade. If several people arrived at the same time, she would take their details and call them back for a private interview in order to collect the rents without arousing the attention of others.

The next day, as she was about to go to the appointment, she noticed a piece of clothing hanging from the hook in the entrance. It was a red and white "hounds tooth" raincoat that Sabine had left at home during one of her surprise visits.

Carmen smiled at the idea of a new trick. She put on the garment, put on her nose with tinted glasses and let the long brown hair that she usually wore in a ponytail float over her shoulders.

A quick look at the large wall mirror, the similarity was perfect. If asked, people would swear they recognized Sabine!

The affair was carried out with a bang. Carmen had the good fortune to see the buyers parade at regular intervals. She distributed the keys, specifying that boxing would be free on Friday morning, and collected the deposits. Of course, there were more checks than cash, but that was an eventuality she had expected.

When the evening came, she threw away the checks, counted the bills and found that she had a pretty tidy sum. She called Diego to let him know that she would be on the road the next morning. She would be at his house by the end of the evening.

On his return, Sylvain would manage with the cheated tenants. He didn't even know Diego's hotel existed, he would never find it again!

*****

Not a free parking spot and the rain that didn't stop. Sylvain spotted Carmen's car and double-parked next to her. That way he wouldn't bother anyone. He turned off the headlights, cut the ignition.

- Wait for me here. I'll take your raincoat and I'll be right back downstairs," he said, turning to Sabine.

They had cut short their stay in Fontainebleau because the weather had turned and Sabine absolutely wanted to get her "hounds tooth" raincoat back.

She had plenty of other rain gear, but that night, that was the one she wanted to wear! Sylvain was used to his friend's whims and thought it was precisely this spoiled child side that made her so charming.

"A sacred temperament" he thought while running towards the entrance of the building. Definitely, this girl set his blood on fire, quite the opposite of Carmen! Although the sweetness of her companion is not to displease him either. It was restful.

- In short, two beautiful girls whose characters complement each other, that's the perfect situation, he said to himself, smiling.

Carmen had gone to bed early, but too nervous to sleep, she got up immediately. Her suitcase being already packed, she had decided that it was best to leave without further delay.

After a quick shower she checked one last time that she hadn't forgotten anything. The rain pattered against the bay window of the living room, she thought it would not be very pleasant to drive at night, in the rain. But at that moment, nothing could have dampened her joy. She grabbed her suitcase.

In front of the apartment door, Sylvain was still smiling as he reached into his pocket to extract his keys. Carefully, he slid the lock.

- Above all, not waking up Carmen, that would make quite a fuss! he says to him.

He pushed open the door, which slid silently. His smile faded from his lips.

Carmen was there, in front of him, a travel bag slung over her shoulder, a suitcase in her hand.

Both remained frozen in surprise for a few moments.

- But what does that mean? stammered Sylvain. What are you doing here with those suitcases?

- I'm leaving, she replied simply.

- Are you leaving? How are you leaving?

For a bit, he would have stuttered! Choked, he pushed the young woman back inside. So she wanted to leave him! He had thought her submissive, at his mercy, and she dared to leave without telling him!

Calling on all her courage, Carmen stood straight in front of him.

- Let me through, Sylvain. I'm leaving and that's it.

She took a step forward. Sylvain shoved her away again. A vague whiff of love mingled with the anger that overwhelmed him. But his violent temper took over.

- You won't leave me, like that, without explanation, he cried, beside himself, trying to grab her.

Carmen was not determined to let herself go, although terrified, she resisted him with all her might. Losing all control, he slapped her so hard that the travel bag slipped off the young woman's shoulder and fell heavily to the floor.

A second slap. Carmen backed away quickly to try to escape the blows, the heel of her shoe caught in the strap of the bag lying at her feet. Her eyes filled with fear, she tried to regain her balance.

Sylvain saw her go backwards, he didn't have time to make a move, like in a film shot in slow motion, and he saw her head hit the frame of the living room door.

His anger subsided immediately, giving way to fear. Carmen was no longer moving and the fixity in her gaze did not bode well. He approached the lifeless body fearfully and strained himself to feel its pulse. Not the slightest pulse.

- It's not my fault, he murmured to reassure himself I didn't do it on purpose. She was the one who looked for him!

But already images of the police, assize courts and prison were jostling in his head. Distraught, he looked around him, desperately looking for a lifeline. Suddenly, a name came to mind "Sabine" He was sure, Sabine would know what to do! He rushed to the stairwell.

At first glance, the young woman grasps the gravity of the situation.

- No need to call an ambulance, she's dead, there's no doubt! She said without losing her composure.

- But then what are we going to do? Sylvain asked, ready to let her take matters into her own hands.

- We can call the police but it may not be the best solution.

- It's an accident, she fell!

- And you think they'll take your word for it? She retorted. Not to mention that they may take the opportunity to put their noses in our business!

- So what are we going to do? He questioned again.

Staring hard, brow furrowed in concentration, Sabine was pacing through the living room.

- I have an idea! She said suddenly.

He looked at her, full of hope.

- Is it her car that is parked at the foot of the building? Asked the young woman.

- Yes.

- We must deal with the most urgent. We stick her in her trunk with all her luggage and we're off to shove it all in your box. With this cold duck, it will keep like in a fridge! That'll save us some time.

- What's next?

- Afterwards, we are looking for a quiet place. We will find a lake to get rid of the car without being seen. In the meantime, you will spread the rumor that she has gone back to Spain. Besides, that's certainly what she intended to do!

That was the whole funeral oration to which poor Carmen was entitled. No sooner said than done, the old Seat and its macabre load were put back in the box.

The very day after this dismal expedition, Sylvain and Sabine set off in search of the ideal place which would serve as the final burial place for the young Spaniard.

*****

Diego couldn't wait any longer, he was so happy with the hope of seeing his sister again! Usually, he was not of an anxious temperament but, this time, he felt in spite of himself the concern gaining him.

A sort of presentiment mixed with the spontaneous antipathy he had always felt for Sylvain made him imagine the worst.

Two long days had passed since Carmen's phone call. He himself had telephoned Paris several times, without obtaining an answer. He had then made inquiries with the authorities, both Spanish and French.

He had called all the hospitals. There were no accidents to report, no casualties that matched his sister's description. Diego was not a man to sit agonizing over it without reacting.

He prepared a light luggage, entrusted the hotel to his assistant and took the road to Paris. He had no battle plan, he would advise on the spot.

Arriving in Paris, despite his strong-willed character, he felt a bit lost. In vain, he had rung several times at Carmen's door; he had scoured the whole neighborhood but had obtained very little information. The baker thought Carmen had gone back to Spain. Nothing more.

Working from a very young age in tourism, he believed himself to be perfectly multilingual but, in these very special circumstances, he was forced to admit that his French left something to be desired and did not allow him to take his career any further. Investigation.

He went to the police station where he was given little hope. His sister was of legal age and everything suggested that she had returned to the country. So what to do? Go home and wait? He couldn't bring himself to resign himself to it.

- Something bad happened to Carmen, he kept repeating to himself. She wouldn't have left me without news, that's impossible.

At the end of the day, completely demoralized and tired from the long journey he had made, he decided to take a hotel room. In the morning, he called Spain where, of course, he was told that Carmen had given no sign of life.

It was then that he came up with the idea of contacting a private detective agency. He borrowed a directory and began to consult the yellow pages. Right away, in the long list, he spotted the "Alvarez" agency, whose Spanish sound, reminding him of the sun of his country, gave him a little hope.

When the secretary introduced him to the director's office, he was a little surprised, almost disappointed. He had imagined meeting a kind of Mike Hammer and he found himself face to face with a pretty blonde with the face of an angel. She stood up to greet him.

Her handshake was firm and her smile warm. Diego forgot his pre-conceptions and, encouraged by the kindness of the young woman, he confided his fears to her and told her everything he knew about his sister, Sylvain, their life in Paris.

Unlike the police inspectors, Sophie Alvarez seemed to take his story very seriously and assured him that she was immediately on the case.

He left her office slightly comforted. She had promised him that she would call him at the hotel as soon as she had any news. He didn't have to wait long; she called in the early afternoon.

- I got information from notarial offices, she told him. No clerk named Sylvain Favier! Are you sure he works in Paris?

- I'm not sure of anything about him but he always told me he was a clerk in an important Parisian office. I don't know him very well, but each time I've met him, he's talked to me about real estate transactions.

- Real estate transactions? Reminds me of a case we handled recently.

- Another disappearance?

- No, a scam. A case of false notary. Do not leave your hotel, I will call you back! She said before hanging up.

Sophie Alvarez was a good detective. She had a job and a fairly sure intuition. And, precisely, this intuition whispered to her that there could well be a relationship between this untraceable notary's clerk and the case of fraud on which her firm had been plowing for several months. She set about going through the file. She thus noted that the description of the plaintiffs, concerning the false notary, corresponded completely to that of Sylvain.

Encouraged by this discovery, she had the latest newspapers brought to her, trying to locate an advertisement that would recall the case.

All these offers seemed honest but Sophie was stubborn. The anxiety she had read in Diego's dark eyes had moved her deeply.

However, she was beginning to get discouraged when her gaze fell on a stall for rent from the Langlois agency. This name was among the phantom agencies in his file.

- It may be a simple coincidence, she said to herself. Langlois is a very banal surname!

The address was on the ad. For the sake of conscience, she decided to go take a look. Anyway, she had no other leads. She called Diego to offer to accompany her.

*****

It was at the end of a narrow cul-de-sac, a small block of concrete made up entirely of stalls. Three men were talking vehemently there. Sophie and Diego quickened their pace.

In front of the open box, Diego's heart leaps in his chest. Seeing the old Seat registered in Spain, Sophie immediately understood. She took out her mobile phone and called Commissioner Monnier who was in charge of the fraud case.

While waiting for the arrival of the police, the three men explained how they had rented this box to a dark-haired woman dressed in a red and white printed raincoat. Diego, meanwhile, his eyes riveted on his sister's car felt the anxiety invade him.

Commissioner Monnier finally arrived, accompanied by two of his men. They collected the testimonies and decided to inspect the car. When they opened the safe, Diego couldn't hold back his tears. Sophie held out her hand, which he grabbed and squeezed in his own.

It was this moment that Sylvain and Sabine chose to make their appearance. The day before, they had unearthed a small muddy pond that suited their sinister purposes.

Sabine was wearing her red and white raincoat and Sylvain was whistling as he twirled the keys to Carmen's car around his index finger.

In front of the police grouped around the open trunk, they tried to turn back. But the sight of firearms pointed at them dissuaded them.

End

Also By The Author in Children Short Story Series:

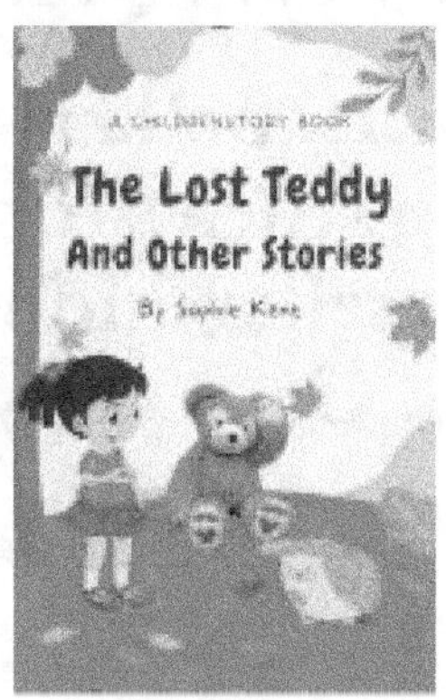

Get it Here: https://www.amazon.com/dp/B09YL8X3KF

Get Your Copy Here: https://kdp.amazon.com/amazon-dp-

action/us/
dualbookshelf.marketplacelink/
B09Y7NQ1RS

A Challenge for Isabella is a collection of three interesting stories for children. This book is a bestseller and very popular among children. Get a copy for your child too.